EBB & FLOW

EBB & FLOW

Heather Smith

Kids Can Press

Kids Can Press gratefully acknowledges the financial support of the Government of Ontario, through the Ontario Media Development Corporation; the Ontario Arts Council; the Canada Council for the Arts; and the Government of Canada for our publishing activity.

Published in Canada and the U.S. by Kids Can Press Ltd.
25 Dockside Drive, Toronto, ON M5A 0B5

Kids Can Press is a Corus Entertainment Inc. company

www.kidscanpress.com

Edited by Yasemin Uçar
Designed by Julia Naimska
Cover illustration by Kenard Pak

Printed and bound in Altona, Manitoba, Canada, in 11/2018 by Friesens Corp.

CM 18 0 9 8 7 6 5 4 3

Library and Archives Canada Cataloguing in Publication

Smith, Heather, 1968–, author
　　Ebb and flow / written by Heather Smith.
ISBN 978-1-77138-838-2 (hardcover)
　　I. Title.

PS8637.M5623E23 2018　　jC813'.6　　C2017-903189-9

For April, a gem of a girl — H.S.

Summer

One summer,
after a long plane ride
and a rotten bad year,
I went to Grandma Jo's.
It was my mother's idea.
Jett, what you need is a change of scenery.
I think *she* needed a change of scenery, too.
One without me.
Because that rotten bad year?
That was my fault.
I wondered if a summer spent
in a little wooden house
on a rocky eastern shore
would help us forget that.

As the plane flew across
the blue-green ocean,
I crossed my fingers
and hoped.

Turbulence

Inside,
I was flipping
and flopping,
churned up
like the rough sea
below.

PLEASE FASTEN YOUR SEAT BELTS FOR LANDING.

There it was.
The place I was taken from
when Dad went to jail.

Grandma Jo

I remembered
her house was painted pink,
a sugary, pastel shade
she said made her heart sing,
a shade she loved so much
she dyed her hair to match.
She called herself
the cotton candy granny.

I remembered
hugs that were big for her size,
her arms growing
like expandable straws.
The tighter they got,
the smaller I felt.

As I walked off the plane
I wondered
if a big kid like me
could feel small in her arms again.

The Old Me

I wondered if she'd be expecting the old me.
I hoped not.
The old me was dead.

Small Again

She pushed through the crowd,
shouting,
Yoo-hoo! Jett!
but when she got close
she stopped.

Jett, I can't decide
if you're the bee's knees
or the cat's pajamas.

I buried my face in her jacket,
a sweet-smelling rainbow of fleece.
I was Jett the Incredible Shrinking Boy,
small in her arms again.

She asked if I liked her hair,
a cotton-candy blue.

Your house, too?

She nodded.

She was crazy, my grandma.
My cotton candy granny.

Joanna

Her lime-green car
had no back seat
and a trunk
the size of a bread box.
She put my suitcase on the roof.
Fisherman's knots. Watch closely.
But her little old hands
went faster than I expected
and I was no good
at remembering,
which is why I did so bad at school.

We drove for lots of minutes,
an hour's worth or more,
but Grandma's stories
made the minutes feel like seconds.
Stories about Joanna,
a funny little girl
who believed in fairies
and spent her free time
skipping stones.
(Her record was ten.)
Joanna was Grandma Jo,
I knew that,
but I liked the way she said *she* and *her*
as if she was a book character.

Later, Grandma said,
What about you, Jett?
Do you have any stories to tell?

I shook my head
because in my stories I wasn't a hero.
I was a villain.

Pounding

As we pulled up
to the little wooden house
on the rocky eastern shore
my heart went crazy,
pounding,
like the crashing waves
I could hear in the distance.
I was so happy to be back,
I almost forgot
I was there to forget.

Marshmallows Straight from the Bag

We ate fish and chips
drowned in vinegar
and washed it all down
with some soda.
We had
greasy fingers,
salty lips,
full bellies.
We ate till all that was left
was ketchup streaked on the plate,
like finger paint,
messy and wild.

Then,
marshmallows
straight from the bag,
white as clouds,
light as air,
one after another
until, *poof*,
they were gone,
every last one.

Marmaduke

She gave me the room in the attic,
the one with the view of the sea.
Of all the rooms
in all the world
it was the awesomest room
of them all.
It made me feel cozy
and glow-y
and warm,
like a light had turned on
in my heart.

Instead of a bedside table,
there was a man made out of wood.
Big nose,
big ears,
cheeks that drooped
down his face.

Grandma said,
Meet my new butler.
His name's Marmaduke.
His tray can hold all your books.

I said,
I only read comics.

She said,
What's a comic if it's not a book?

I thought,
But it's barely got words.

Quilt of a Million Squares

There was a quilt on the bed
made of a million squares
and the pillows were
frilly and plump.

Two pillows
for a one-person bed.

Both of them for me.

The Bear

There was a bear on a chair
in the corner
that made my heart-light
go dim.

You okay, Jett?

He reminded me of Alf,
that was all.
Alf and my rotten bad year.

Old Times

You don't like the bear?

He's kinda creepy.
I'll BEARly sleep tonight.
Get it, Grandma? BEARly?

I get it, Jett. I get it.

Are you PAWSitive?
Because you're not laughing.

I'm not laughing,
because that joke was unBEARable.

It was just like old times.
(Puns were our thing.)

Go to bed, Jett. You're driving me BEARserk!

Alone in the room,
I BEARied the bear

deep, deep, deep

in the closet.

They Came Quick, the Feelings

They came like a downpour of rain.

Fast,
hard,
out of the blue.

If only they came like mist instead.

Mist can't soak you to the bones.

Shell

I said to the butler,
Okay if I call you Duke?

I imagined him saying,
Please do.

I asked,
Are you hollow?
Because I felt hollow,
like an egg
with the insides blown out,

a shell holding air.

Counting Waves

I pulled the quilt
up under my chin
and let the whoosh of the sea
fill my head.

*Duke, let's count waves
like we're counting sheep.*

Together we started at one.
On whoosh number twelve,
a knock at the door.

*Jett?
I just wanted to say
I'm glad you are here.*

And all of a sudden,
I was more than just air.

Sea Glass

I followed her
along the water's edge.
What are you doing?

Hunting.

For fish?

Her laugh was always bigger
than I expected.

She combed the shore
in blue rubber boots,
peering here and there
between the rocks.
Then,
a fist pump.
Yes!

It was the size of a pebble,
frosty, round and smooth.
Red, she said. *A rare one.*

Grandma Jo,
Sea Glass Hunter.

Starfish

All I found was a starfish.
Pink,
bumpy,
a piece missing
from one of its arms.
Or were they legs?
I wasn't sure.

I felt sad,
which was weird.
It was only a starfish.
Did it even have feelings?

For the first time in forever
I thought I might cry.

Seemed I cared more
about that starfish
than I did about
all that happened
that rotten bad year.

The Crouching Lion

On the shoreline
there was a lion,
tame enough
to be climbed,
wild enough
to play with the waves.

Careful, Jett!
That boulder will be an island at high tide.

Good,
then I will stay here
until I get stranded.
The water will get
higher and higher
and no one will be able to reach me,
to save me,
and I will deserve it.
I will deserve to be stranded
on an island
all by myself.

The waves lapped softly
at the lion's feet.

Shhhhhhhh
Shhhhhhhh
Shhhhhhhh

If I was a wave I'd come in with a crash,
no matter how hard I tried to roll.

All This Stuff in My Head

Grandma climbed to the top of the lion.
(She was always stronger than I expected.)

You okay?

I have all this stuff in my head.

Maybe this fresh air will clear it.

I breathed in.

Maybe.

Five Pieces

In Grandma's hand,
five pieces of sea glass —
two white, two green,
one red.

I didn't find anything, I said.

You will.

Alf

My mother called from the mainland.
I saw Alf at McEwan's store.

Did he mention me?

Oh, well, no, you see ...

I put the phone down
with no goodbyes.

Sitting on the crouching lion,
I tried to forget,
but there it was,
everywhere I looked,
Alf's face —
sweet and round and covered in stubble.

The Mainland

Mom had called it our fresh start,
but it felt like the end of something,

until I met Junior Dawson.

He was a big kid,
freckled,
his blond hair fluffy,
like a baby bird's feathers.

He had big hands,
hands that hit.
A punch in the arm,
a smack on the head.

The smirks I gave him
were a secret code:
I feel like hitting someone, too.

It wasn't long till he cracked the code
and let me be his friend.

Scrabble

On a day when the call of the beach
was muffled by the rain on the windows,
Grandma placed a game between us.
She said,
I'll take score,
because it was a well-known fact
that numbers and me
didn't get along too good.
What she didn't know,
or maybe she did,
was that letters and me
didn't get along, either.

Our game of Scrabble was doomed from the start.

Dumb

When Grandma laid words

like JICAMA
and MUNDANE,
I bit my lip
and wrinkled my nose.
It was a habit
I never knew I had
till Junior said,
You look as dumb as my uncle Alf.

Sometimes, I really hated Junior.

Shrinking Words

Grandma started using
her words in a sentence.
You look perplexed
by the word PERPLEX.
I bit my lip
until I tasted
blood.

The words I laid
were silly and small.
DOG
SHIP
AS
LOG.

After a few turns
Grandma's words
started to shrink.
PLUM
YELL
FIN.

Dumbness, it seemed,
was contagious.

I laid PITYING.
A seven-letter word.
(Score some points for the dummy.)

I had a *Q* without a *U*
and way too many *A*s.
I even had a tile
with the letter rubbed off
and I thought,
What the heck
am I supposed to do
with a stupid blank tile?

Grandma laid WISH.
I said,
I don't want to play anymore.

She gathered the tiles.
Your WISH is my command.

Bookshelf Jenga

The next game she wanted
was jammed in the middle
of the stack.
One tug,
and they all fell down.

Fine with me.

The longer it took to clean up,
the longer it was till we had to play.

Monopoly was the worst game in the whole entire world.

Playing Pieces

In the battered old box
there was
an iron, a car, a boot,
a dog, a ship, a hat,
a wheelbarrow, a thimble.

I didn't like any of them.
(Who would choose a stupid thimble?)

Grandma said,
How about the dog?

It looked like Toto.
I never saw
The Wizard of Oz,
but Alf did.
Dorothy's dog
was his favorite.

Alf loved animals.

Grandma rubbed her hands together.
Shall we begin?

I picked up Toto
and put him on GO.
Grandma laid the thimble beside him.

Monopoly Money

Let's count, Jett.
We need two five hundreds,
two one hundreds,
two fifties …

I wished I was at the beach,
where the only numbers
were the ones in my head,
counting,

1, 2, 3, 4 …

waiting for that one wave
to roll in bigger than the rest.

5, 6 …

SWOOSH!

Then, I'd start again.

Jett? Count with me.
Six twenties,
five tens …
What's the total so far?

I looked at the window
as if the drops of rain
would form the answer
on the glass.

They didn't.

Zero

We took turns rolling the dice.
I did what she said:
Buy. Rent. Sell.
I was a robot.
A robot playing Monopoly.
Then I landed on
GO TO JAIL
and my robot-ness disappeared.
I yelled,
I HATE THIS GAME!
and threw the board
onto the floor.
I said a swear word, too,
in a really loud voice.
At least I think I did,
I can't be sure —
madness makes everything fuzzy.
Grandma's mouth looked like an O
or maybe a zero —
a big fat zero like me.

She said,
Why did you do that?

I shrugged.
I guess that's what happens
after a rotten bad year —
one minute you're fine
and the next you're the Hulk.

Smelly Nelly

One day,
Grandma said,
Let's go to Nelly's.
I wasn't sure who she meant.
I only knew one Nelly —
Smelly Nelly —
who begged on the sidewalk
in front of the bank.
We couldn't have been going
to *her* house.
She was homeless.

Nelly had squinty eyes
that looked right through you,
and her nails were long,
like claws.
She only had one tooth
in her whole entire head.
It hung at an angle
over her bottom lip
like a broken board
on a picket fence.
No, we couldn't be going to see
Smelly Nelly.
That would be weird.

A Conversation

Do I have to go?

I visit Nelly Peddle once a week
and while you're staying with me,
you will, too.

Isn't she homeless?

She rents a room at a boardinghouse now.

Where did she get the money?

Jett, do you know what killed the cat?

What a curious question — a dog?

Don't make me laugh, Jett. Not while I'm driving.

The Man Asleep on the Step

If there was one thing
I was good at,
it was noticing stuff.
The man asleep on the step had

a bottle in his hand that said *vodka*
a cut on the side of his cheek
a hole in the butt of his pants.

Junior would have said,
Get a job, loser.

But how can you get a job
when there's a hole
in the butt
of your pants?

The Dump

A long time ago,
on a hot day in July,
Dad and me went
to the dump.

Dad slid the mattress
off the truck.
You take this end, I'll take the other.

I didn't breathe
till I was back in the car.

Nelly's house
smelled like that day,
like trash
getting baked in the sun.

The Man in Number Six

I wasn't a smart kid,
but I knew that the backward C
on Nelly's door
was really a five
with the top knocked off.

Yoo-hoo, Nelly!
Five didn't open,
but six did,
wide enough
for two darting eyes.

Sey are comink.

His words were heavy,
like each one was strapped
with a ten-ton weight.

Who's coming?
asked Grandma.

Aliens.

There are no aliens here, love.
I can promise you that.

The door to number six
clicked shut.

Nelly

Yoo-hoo, Nelly!

Behind the door,
shuffling.

Nelly, dear!

I was about to say,
Let's go,
but the door opened,
so I swallowed the words
instead of speaking them.

For most people,
losing teeth
would make you look worse,
but Nelly looked better
with her one tooth gone —
even when she smiled
and her lips
got sucked
deep inside her mouth.

Nelly had a hump
like a camel
and walked with a limp.
If Junior had seen her he'd have laughed,
and if I was with Junior
I'd have laughed, too.

Moving Dust

There was only one chair
in that stinky room,
in that stinky house,
and Nelly gave it to me.
It was blue
with metal legs.
White fluff
stuck out from a split
in the vinyl seat.

I said,
That's okay, I'll stand.

Grandma said,
*You sit, Jett. Nelly and I
have some things to do.*

So I sat
while Grandma looked
through Nelly's cupboards
making *tut-tut* sounds.
Oh, Nelly.

The wooden floor
was covered in dust
and sometimes
the dust moved,
like it was alive.

I thought,
*Even with a hump on your back
you can sweep the floors.*

A List for Nelly

Grandma was making a list.
Butter, bread, apples …
You don't like apples?
Oranges?
Okay, oranges.
Eggs, cheese, milk …

I went to the window
and finished the list
in my head:
a broom
a duster
some teeth
a life.

I never used to be so mean.

A glass paperweight sat on the windowsill.
Inside, a thousand colors swirled together,
like melted crayons.
I slipped it into my pocket.
I don't know why.

When we were leaving, Nelly grabbed my hand.
Gob besh you.

Her fingers were colder than ice.

When People with No Teeth Made Me Sad

That night,
as I lay in bed,
I sucked my lips
in over my teeth
and spoke out loud
in the dark.
Gob besh you.

I tried again.
Gob besh you.

Gob besh you.
Gob besh you.
Gob besh you.

Stupid Nelly.
All she had to do
was brush her teeth.
If she'd brushed her teeth,
maybe she'd have a job
and live in a house
with more than one chair.

Gob besh you.

She only offered me
her ugly old chair
because she knew
she'd be standing
with Grandma.

Alf offered me
his last piece of
licorice once.
I put my arm around him
and squeezed
his shoulder.
No, Alf, that's yours. You eat it.

That was a long time ago,
when I was a good person,
when people with no teeth
made me sad.

Thud

I took the paperweight
out from under the bed
and tossed it,
hand to hand,
like a baseball.
I said to Duke,
Don't waste your time
being my friend.
I'm a thief.
Back and forth,
back and forth,
the paperweight went
until it fell with a thud
to the floor.

Gob dammit.

Questions

Alf had big eyes
that moved around slowly
like he was seeing things
for the very first time.
His eyes asked questions
that I always answered.
That's a dragonfly, Alf.
That's a transport truck.
Don't worry, Alf. That's just a car backfiring.

Nelly's eyes asked questions, too.
Why are you afraid of me?
Why don't you like me?
Nelly's questions
I pretended not to see.

Flowerpot

One morning, after a sea glass hunt
(Grandma: 4, me: 0),
Grandma pulled a chocolate bar
out of her pocket
and said,
Want to hear a Joanna story?
She didn't wait for an answer.
She broke the bar in half
and began:

*This one's called
"Joanna and the Baby Doll."
One Christmas,
when Joanna was five,
Santa gave her a baby doll
with red rosy cheeks
and pinkish pursed lips.
Joanna called her
Flowerpot.
Funny name, I know,
but Joanna was a funny girl.
Still is.
Anyway, one day,
Joanna noticed a hole
between Flowerpot's lips.
So in through that hole
went milk-soaked bread,
yogurt,
cottage cheese
and,
most of all,
because it was
Flowerpot's favorite,
custard.*

One day,
Joanna's mother said,
"What's that smell?"
She sniffed here
and there
and everywhere
until her nose
found Flowerpot.
Poor Flowerpot —
she got thrown in the trash.

Next Christmas,
Santa brought Joanna another doll.
There was no wee little hole
between pinkish pursed lips.
Not right away, anyway.
It took three days
for Joanna to force
her mother's darning needle
through the tough,
rubbery plastic.
Luckily,
Flowerpot the Second
was allergic to dairy
and ate biscuit crumbs instead.

Grandma said,
Did you like my Flowerpot story?
I said yes,
even though it reminded me of Alf.

Alf's Doll

Alf had a doll.
It wore a policeman's uniform.
Alf called him Tective.
Alf loved policemen.
Too bad he was crying
when he finally met one.

Catchphrase

Mom asked me once
if I regretted what I did.
I lied and said no.

Junior and me,
we had a catchphrase:
NO REGRETS.

It was like one of those
bouncy safety nets
that firefighters held
at the bottom of burning buildings —
whenever I felt like I was falling
I'd whisper NO REGRETS
and I'd bounce so high
I'd fly through the sky
and lose myself
in the clouds.

But, in the end,
when I needed it most,
the safety net
wasn't there.

Reflection

Grandma massaged her head
with foamy blue suds.
Want some?

I smiled.
Cotton candy Jett.

My hair is too dark. It won't show up.

Then we'll bleach it first.

The peroxide tingled my nose.

That's why they called you Jett, you know.
It means dark-haired.

She held up a mirror.
I jumped at my reflection.

I guess I'll have to change my name now.

Grandma added blue
to my white spiked bangs.
How about Ocean or Sky?

If I was named Sky
I wouldn't have done what I did,
because Junior Dawson
would never have been
friends with someone named Sky.

Grandma said,
Want to see your new look?

I'm DYEing to.
Get it, Grandma? DYEing?

I get it, Jett. I get it.

I looked in the mirror.
A kid with cool blue hair looked back.

If I'd known it was that easy to become someone new,
I'd have dyed my hair on the mainland.

Up

Grandma and me
stood in the cold,
choosing between
two movies.
I liked the poster on the left.
It was full of explosions.
Grandma liked the one on the right.
It was full of balloons.

Let's see Up,
she said.
(That was the one with balloons.)

I'm too old for cartoons,
I said.

Grandma said,
I'm too old for explosions.

No Words

In the opening scene,
a guy and a girl
were falling in love.
There were no words,
just music.
I liked that.
Words would just make
the love story gross.

The guy and the girl
got married.

Then,
there was a baby.

Then,
there wasn't.

It was a rotten bad year
for that guy and that girl.

But they stayed in love
until they got old.
Real old.

We knew what was coming.
The whole audience did.
It was like someone stuck
a giant straw in the theater
and sucked all the air out.

Grandma was sniffing
and my chest got tight,
and when the old lady
up on the screen
was lying in a hospital bed

and the old man next to her
looked empty and sad,
I thought,
What kind of cartoon is this?

Bad Thing

After the movie
we went out to eat.
I sat in the booth
of the old-fashioned diner
staring at the seeds
on my hamburger bun.
Grandma said,
That was a real tearjerker, huh?
And I said,
I did a bad thing this year.
Grandma said,
I know.

A Conversation

There are visiting days at the penitentiary, you know.

What do you care? He's nothing to you.

He's my daughter's husband. That's something.

Well, your daughter doesn't want me to see him.
That's why she took me to the mainland.

Well, she's not here, is she?

Thanks for reminding me!

She thought the break would be good, that's all.

Yeah. For her.

Mom

I was her smoochums,
her sugar,
her sweetheart,
her love.

Till I met Junior.

Then,
I was trouble,
a problem,
a nuisance,
a thug.

When I met Junior, all the "hers" disappeared.

I was an "a" belonging to no one.

Penitentiary

Douglas Campbell, aged 38,
sentenced to Her Majesty's Penitentiary.

That's what the paper said.
Penitentiary.
Why couldn't they just say *jail*
or *prison*?
It didn't really matter,
I supposed.
All I knew was
it was the place you went
when you drank too much
and drove your car
on New Year's Eve.

Dad

The people that called him "sir"
would never have guessed
that my dad,
the banker,
would end up in jail.

He said,
I'm not a drunk.
I only drink on special occasions.

As if that made it okay.

New Year's Eve
must have been extra special.

Diseased

When the news came out
it was like I had a disease —
a gross, scabby, rashy disease
that you could catch
if you came anywhere near me.
That's why,
at my new school,
I made friends
with Junior Dawson.
He'd think
having a father in jail
was the coolest disease
in the world.
Not that I planned on telling him.
But if it came out,
I figured he'd have my back.

Becoming his friend
was super easy.
When he swore,
I swore.
When he laughed,
I laughed.
And whenever he smacked
Colby McKenzie,
I'd laugh extra loud
and words I'd never said before
would pour from my mouth,
real easy,
like milk into a glass.

That's the thing
about being someone new —
once you kill your old self
and bury it deep underground
it'll never come back,

no matter how hard you dig.

The Big Glass Fish

One day Grandma said,
Jett, let's paint this room electric purple,
and I said,
Sure,
as if she'd suggested
a walk on the beach
or a cup of tea.
Nothing surprised me
about Grandma anymore.
Just the day before, she'd said,
Now how about we run a comb over Horace?
Horace was her stuffed puffin.
He was real once.
I tried not to think about that
as I combed his feathers
and looked into his beady black eyes.

Grandma passed me a box.

Clear off the window ledge, would you?
The last thing I want is a purple-plumaged puffin.

One by one, I took down
a naked lady statue,
a porcelain cat wearing a red beret,
a doll inside a doll inside a doll inside a doll,
some fairies,
some fossils,
a whale bone.

The last thing to move was a glass fish —
big mouth,
big tail,
a belly full of sea glass.

It was heavy in my hands
and as I moved it,
it caught the light,

a kaleidoscope of colors.

Alf's voice,
a happy memory in my head.

Klido-scope. Klido-scope.

Then, a not-so-happy one.

Jett not my friend anymore.

I raised the fish as high
as my arms would stretch,
then ...

I let go.

Klido-scope

Once, at a school fair,
I won a kaleidoscope.
All I had to do
was burst three balloons
with a dart.

I gave my prize to Alf.

He looked through the eyepiece
and said,
Broken window.

I wasn't sure why.

Then, one day,
a walk past St. Mary's Church.

Klido-scope. Klido-scope.

Above the door,
a stained-glass window,
made from a thousand colored pieces.

Klido-scope. Klido-scope.

Like She Meant It

I thought she'd be mad,
but her mouth was a smile.

Phew! For a minute there I thought you'd hurt yourself.

Was she for real?
Your fish.

She shrugged.
Accidents happen.

But ... your fish.

It was smashed to smithereens.

It's okay.

No, it's not.

Yes, it is.

No, it's not.

Yes. It is.

The way she said it
Like. She. Meant. It.
made me believe

it *was* okay.

Then,
I did the thing
I hadn't done
since my father left,
silver handcuffs
around his wrists:

I cried.

Grandma knelt beside me,
her arms around me tight,
listening
to the squeaks and the gulps
of my cries trapped inside.

She said,
Let it out, Jett.

So I did.

All That Battering

Piece by piece
she filled my hands
with the sea glass.

Teal
Emerald
Olive
Cornflower, my favorite.

When my hands were full
I slipped the glass
into a brown paper bag
and we started again.

This one's from the fifties, she said.

It was golden brown,
shiny and bubbly,
like a big drop of maple syrup.

How do you know?

See the letters?

I squinted. *C-L-O.*

It's from an old Clorox bleach bottle —
they stopped making them like this in the sixties.

How did it get in the ocean?

Someone threw it on the beach, I guess,
and the broken pieces got taken out to sea.

I ran my fingers over the edges.

It's so smooth.

It got quite a bashing,
that little piece of glass.

It spent years
caught in the ocean waves.
It was tossed around
and beaten down,
until finally
it washed up on shore.
Now look at it —
what was once a piece
of broken glass
is now something better —
it's a gem.

Even after all that battering?

Grandma smiled.
Because of all that battering.

Love Me Do

We painted all day,
The Beatles in the background.
Grandma sang along to "Love Me Do"
and I hummed with her,
amazed at how quickly
and easily
the walls turned
from boring beige
to purple.

No battering required.

Like Father, Like Son

We were leaning against
the drugstore wall,
waiting.
Waiting for someone
to look our way
so Junior could say,
What are you looking at?
But no one dared,
not since Danny Young
answered, *Not much,*
and got a shove
that broke his wrist
in three places.

Junior said,
Let's steal a Coke.

I didn't say no.

Why would I?
We were tough guys
and tough guys
stole Coke.
(At least I supposed they did,
when they got thirsty
and had no money.)

Junior said,
*You wanna do it
or will I?*

I shrugged.
I'll do it.

If *I* got caught
they could say,
Like father,
like son.

Junior would have
no excuse at all.

Here Comes the Lunatic

I brushed past Junior,
hoping his toughness
would rub off on me.

At the ding of the bell,
Mr. McEwan looked up.
Can I help you?

Do you have any Coke?

He looked at me like I was dumb.
(Which I was.)

Over in the cooler.

How much is it?

Price is on the door.

I made a show of patting my pockets.

Darn. No money. How 'bout an IOU?
You know, I take the Coke
and bring the money back later?

His jaw went hard.
How 'bout you get the hell out?

Outside, I acted out of breath.
Got caught, but he let me go.

Junior looked suspicious.
Funny, I didn't even see you go to the cooler.

Then,
out of nowhere,
shouting.
Look! Look!

Here comes the lunatic,
said Junior.

Running straight for me,
a man.

Look! Look!

I backed up
against the drugstore wall.

The lunatic grabbed my arm.
Look! Look!

My heart was pounding.
Look at what?

Then, I saw it.
A brown moth,
papery and small,
clinging to the big man's shirt.

He smiled.
Beautiful butterfly.

And just like that,
I wasn't scared anymore.
Not one bit.

Uncles

I let the moth crawl
onto my hand
and held it up
to the light.
Pretty, isn't it?

His mouth was splattered
with foamy spit.
I like butterflies.

Junior's mouth was mean.
Go home, Uncle Retard.
You're gross.

I had an uncle once.
He had legs that didn't work.
Sometimes, he drooled.
We watched *Toy Story* together
twenty-seven times.

His name was Winston.
I loved him till the day that he died.
Then I loved him some more.

Best Friend

Junior yelled,
Are you listening to me, Alf?

Alf put his hands over his ears.

Are you deaf? I said, go home!

Alf looked confused.
I'm not deaf.

As far as I was concerned,
being mean to someone
who doesn't understand
makes being mean
a whole lot meaner.
So I looked Junior
right in the eye
and said,
Leave him alone.

Junior snorted.
He's your best friend now, is he?

Alf stretched his arms out wide.

I glared at Junior and walked into them.

Hugging is something everyone can understand.

Introduction

I said,
My name's Jett.

Jett Plane!

Junior rolled his eyes.
Hey, Uncle Alf,
go take a Coke from McEwan's cooler.

No, I said. *Don't.*

Don't worry. If he gets caught
McEwan will just give it to him.

Still. It's teaching him to steal.

Well, I want a Coke and I don't have money.

I have money, said Alf.
I'm rich.

Shut up, dummy. We're poor as dirt
and everyone knows it.

I'm not poor.
I have lots and lots of money.

Junior's eyes
were getting squinty and mean
and I didn't want him
to use the R-word again,
so I ran home
as fast as I could
and took five dollars,
quick as a wink,
from my mother's purse.

Still ...

Alf downed his drink
in one long gulp,
then wandered away
down the road.

I called,
without thinking,
Be careful!

Junior frowned.
Why'd you say that?

I dunno ...
I just wonder ...
Should he be out on his own?

Jeez, Jett. He's like forty years old.

Alf's "butterfly" swirled round my head.

Yeah,
I said.
Still ...

Pretend

I saw him everywhere
after that.
In the park,
at the store,
outside school.

Wandering,
wondering,
waiting.

Waiting for someone to play.

Cops and robbers
was his favorite game.

*Bang bang, Jett Plane,
you're dead.*

Little-kid games
and out-of-breath fun.
The big, little man
and me.

Nelly's Again

I ignored
the clink of her keys,
the zip of her coat,
the snap of her purse.

The only sounds I could hear
were the words from my comics,
alive in my head.

Boom!
Splat!
Kapow!

Sometimes,
if you read hard enough
the whole world disappears.

Jett!

But Grandma could bring the world back quick.

Jett, I said it's time to go to Nelly's.

Her eyes were sharp,
like a hawk's.

Let's. Go.

I nodded, quick,
and ran for my coat,
scurrying,

like a mouse from its prey.

Cabbage Soup

The guy from number six
stirred a pot on the stove.

Grandma took a big sniff.
Smells like heaven.

Grandma's heaven
smelled a lot like hell.

She said,
*A can of tomatoes will
add oomph to your soup.
I'll get you some at the store.*

His eyes went big with surprise.
Sank you. Sank you wery much.

Grandma smiled.
Paz-hal-us-ta.

I guessed that meant "you're welcome."
I guessed she'd looked it up.

Grandma was a better person
than I'd ever be.

What She Wants

Nelly didn't answer
after five loud knocks
so Grandma walked right in.

Nelly, you should keep this door locked.

Nelly just stared at the floor.

Nelly?

When she looked up,
her eyes met mine.

Her no-teeth mouth spoke mumbly words.

Go abay.

Fair enough, said Grandma.
See you next time.

Outside, I said,
You can't just leave her.

Grandma zipped up her coat.
That's what she wants.

What she wants, I thought,
is her paperweight back.

Leaks

As we drove to the store
to buy oomph for the soup,
Nelly's words tumbled round in my brain.
They thudded and thumped,
Go abay,
Go abay,
like running shoes
spun in the dryer.

Outside,
a streetlight turned red.
I counted until it turned green.
Then, abracadabra
and alakazam,
the words poofed
right out of my head.
It was a trick
I had learned
that rotten bad year —
my very own vanishing act.
I'd just focus my mind
and count 1, 2, 3 ...
then I'd shut myself off
like a faucet.
It worked really well
in the daytime,
but at nighttime
there'd always be leaks.
Bad thoughts would drip in
and all through the night
I'd wish for
a magical plumber.

Pickle Jar

I looked up from my comics
and saw it —
an old pickle jar
on the ledge.
I thought,
Sea glass shouldn't be
where old pickles have been,
and wished I could
un-smash the fish.
The jar was right next to Horace,
whose eyes
stared fiercely at me.
I said, out loud,
as if he was real,
What are you looking at, bird?
and he said back,
without moving his beak,
Why'd you kill the fish, kid?

They Came Quick, the Feelings

They came like arrows shot from a bow.

Fast,
mean
and straight for the heart.

If only they came like boomerangs instead.

Boomerangs go back where they came from.

The Comics Eater

My comics:
gifts,
treats,
prizes,
surprises.
Bought for her sweetheart,
her sugar,
her love.
Read,
re-read,
dog-eared
and old.
Reminders
of when I was good.

Me:
on the crouching lion,
feeding my comics
to the sea.

Splish
Splish
Splish
Waves lapping them up.
Splish
Splish
Splish
Like an angry beast.
Splish
Splish
Splish
Feeding on the gifts of bad boys.

Apology

She gave me a cucumber rose,
called it her edible art.

Hey, she said,
if I pickled these,
I'd have myself sour flowers.

The petals were papery thin,
moist like a rose in the rain.

I said,
How do you pickle things anyway?

You have to soak them in brine.

Poor Brian.

Grandma's laugh was tinkly,
like bells.

I popped the rose in my mouth.

Sah-ry abow de fish.

Apologizing was easier
with a mouth full of cucumber.

That's okay.

Grandma?

Mm-hmm?

I don't like that stinky old jar,
not for sea glass.

Grandma looked at me
from head to toe.

Don't you know, Jett,
that it's what's on the inside that counts?

Of course I knew that.
I knew Alf.

Nothingness

That night,
under the million-square quilt,
I imagined
my comics
swirling in the ocean,
falling apart
panel by panel,
hardening over time,
like sea glass.

I imagined
Sea Glass Archie
and Sea Glass Batman
washing up on a faraway beach.
In China, maybe,
or England
or France.

I imagined
an old granny
with blue rubber boots
and hair to match,
pumping her fist at her find.
YES!

That's what I imagined,
warm and cozy
in that little wooden house
on the rocky eastern shore.

But in the real world
things fall apart.
Paper dissolves,
washing away
into nothingness.
And so it should.
Because people who break glass fish
don't deserve nice things,
like comics.
All they deserve
is to be hated by everybody,
even by old stuffed birds.

Under the million-square quilt,
I said,
Duke? Do you hate me yet?

Duke stayed silent.

Don't worry, you will.
Everyone else does.

The Library

Too cold for wandering,
wondering
and waiting,
he went to the library instead.

Jett Plane come.

In the kids' section
sitting on cushions,
the big, little man
and me.

What I Learned at the Library

Scorpions use pincers to catch their prey,
turtles can breathe through their butts,
a group of owls is a parliament

and learning with Alf was fun.

Movies

We went to the movies once.
I said,
You'll love The Jungle Book.

We sat in the dark theater
eating popcorn,
waiting.
When the screen lit up
Alf's face did, too.

Ooooooooh.

I loved Alf.

The film started rolling.

No. No. No.

My hand on his arm.
It's okay, Alf.

His hands on his ears.
Too loud. Too loud.

We went to the library
and read the book instead.

Picnic on the Beach

The swoosh of the waves,
the cries of the gulls,
the crunch of potato chips.
Triangle sandwiches,
tomato and cheese,
on bread she'd baked herself.
Sugary tea in her old silver flask,
chocolate cookies to share.

All these things, the ingredients
of what I knew would be
my sweetest-tasting memory
of summer.

Almost Over

Next to the basket, a newspaper.
Let's do the crossword,
said Grandma.
She read the clue out loud.
Time for harvest. Six letters.
I bit my lip
and wrinkled my nose.
A gull laughed *ha, ha, ha.*

Autumn? I said.

Yes! said Grandma.
Then she sighed.
It'll be here before we know it.

Making Time Stand Still

The laughing gull
tried to steal my chips
and the picnic blanket
made my legs itch,
but if I could have
I would have
made time stand still.

The Whale

We held our breath when we saw the spray.
A few seconds later,
it surfaced.

A humpback,
Grandma whispered.

Under again, then,

PFFFSSHHHH

a fountain of mist,

catching the light just right.

Grandma, did you see that?

In the spray, a rainbow.

Then, he was gone.

Grandma?

Mm-hmm?

Want to hear a story?

Jett Story: Part I

Once upon a time
there was a kid named Jett.
He was a pretty good guy
until he moved to the mainland
and met Junior Dawson.
Junior was bad news —
tough, mean,
a real bad influence.
He had these squinty brown eyes
that sometimes looked yellow,
like a demon's.
Junior made Jett
do lots of bad things.

Grandma looked right through me.

Great story …

if you like fairy tales.

The Truth Was

Sometimes, being bad
felt good.
Like the time
Junior and me
ordered ten pizzas
in our teacher's name
and had them sent to the classroom.

Afterward, Junior called me
his partner in crime.

One Morning Before School

Gimme your lunch, Jett.

Again? Why don't you just eat breakfast?

Mind your own business, doofus.

Why don't you just ask your mom —

What mom?

Wait. You don't have a mom?

Mind your own business, doofus.

Swinging

Lunchtimes
spent off school property,
at a playground,
old and run-down.

Overgrown grass,
a rusty old slide,
broken beer bottles in the sand.

A wooden swing,
hung way too high,
initials scraped in the paint.

J.D.

One full hour,
back and forth,
pumping high to the sky.

He'd only stop when I said,
The bell rang,
then we'd slowly head back.

If we went back at all.

Another Joanna Story

After I told my fairy tale
Grandma said,
How about a real story, Jett?

She took a big breath
and began.
When Joanna was twelve —

Like me,
I said.

Grandma laughed.
Not quite.

Almost.

Yes, said Grandma.
Almost.

When Joanna was twelve
she wanted a pair
of white knee-high boots.
All the girls had them.
Joanna didn't normally want
what the other girls had.
Usually,
Joanna marched to the beat
of a different drummer.
But one day,
at recess,
a group of girls surrounded her.
They said her shiny shoes
with the silver buckles
were for babies.

They said,
"We'll let you go
if you say,
'Goo-goo-gaa-gaa.
I want my mama.'"
Joanna did not want to say that.
She wanted to say,
"I like my shoes!"
But that drummer she marched to?
That drummer had marched away
and the only sound I could hear
was the beating of my own heart.

I didn't like
that she switched to "I,"
so I said,
What did Joanna do next?

I said what they wanted me to say, Jett.
Then, I bought those white boots
with the money I'd saved
for my grandmother's birthday.
I'd planned on getting her the wool scarf
she'd admired in a shop window
the month before.
But I bought the boots instead —
boots that pinched my toes
and squeezed my calves,
boots that the girls at school
said didn't suit me.
And my grandmother?
I bought her half a pound of candies
that were too hard for her old teeth.

Well, it's the thought that counts,
right, Grandma?

Grandma gave a little laugh.
Not if it's barely a thought at all.

Well, I love getting candy for gifts.
I bet your grandma did, too.

Grandma smiled with a sad face.
Not getting her that scarf
was one of the biggest regrets
of my life.
See, a few months later,
my grandmother got a cough.
I kept thinking,
maybe a scarf would have helped.

It was just a cough, Grandma. It wasn't your fault.

It turned into pneumonia, Jett.
She died shortly after.

I swallowed a lump
that was stuck in my throat.
Everyone makes mistakes, Grandma.

She looked at me with hawk eyes.

Yes, Jett, they do.

Almost Twelve

Grandma asked if I wanted a party.

A party?
Who would we invite?
Smelly Nelly?
The guy with the hole
in the butt of his pants?
Horace the stupid stuffed puffin?
Even if I was back on the mainland
I wouldn't have a friend
to invite.

We could have a bonfire on the beach,
she said.
Cook up some hotdogs.
Play some board games afterward.

Just me and you?

I wouldn't want to have a party
with anyone else.

Colby McKenzie's Party

Two invitations in the school trash —
Junior fished them out.

Guess who's going to Colby's party?

Not us, I said. *We're not wanted.*

Then why'd he make us invitations?

The whole class got them.

Well, there you go! We're in!

Take a hint, Junior. He threw ours in the garbage.

Tough. We're going. Whether he wants us there or not.

Colby's Room

A desk,
a computer,
a TV,
a gaming system.

That's what was in
Colby's room.

Outside, the other kids,
the ones whose invitations
weren't in the trash,
were where they should be,
on the big front lawn
watching magic tricks.

Inside, Junior was doing magic tricks of his own.

He was making money disappear.

Piggy Bank

It wasn't pink,
like a real pig,
it was blue.

Help me, Jett.

The rubber stopper
was jammed in tight.

*Maybe if you didn't bite your nails
you could do it yourself.*

I ran my nail between the rubber
and the ceramic,
breaking the seal.
One tug,
and the stopper was free.

Most piggy banks
held coins,
but Colby's held
paper money, too.

Junior took one,
then two,
then three
neatly folded
five-dollar bills
out of the pig's belly.

I said,
One more and you'll have twenty.

Twenty dollars,
once Colby's,
now Junior's,
and I didn't care one bit.

Outside, the other kids
were eating trays of sandwiches
and cookies the size of my face.

Inside, Junior was just evening things up.

Mustard Sandwich

He brought a mustard sandwich to school once.

Dang it. My stupid dad forgot the meat.

Junior was like Pinocchio,
except his nose didn't grow,
it wrinkled.
I loved catching him out.

Haha, saw your nose wrinkle, you liar!

But when he lied about his mustard sandwich,
I said nothing.

Present Time

When Colby opened his gifts,
Junior said,
I hate that kid.

When he opened mine,
I said,
It's from Junior, too.

Colby didn't need to see my nose grow
to know I was lying.

Walking home,
Junior said,
That present was really lame.

At least I brought a present.

Sometimes, being mean
was contagious.

As we walked past McEwan's store,
Junior pulled out a five-dollar bill.
Back in a sec. I'm getting a Coke.

*Shouldn't you use that money
to buy meat for your mustard sandwiches?*

Boy, did I have a bad case of meanness.

Junior's face went red.
Shut up, Jett.

Showing Off

He opened his can with a kshhh,
took a long drink,
then laughed
ha ha ha
to himself.

What's so funny?

*Remember when you wimped out
trying to steal a can of Coke?*

*I didn't wimp out.
I got caught.*

Yeah. Sure you did.

Junior made me feel
as lame as the colored markers
I'd chosen for Colby's birthday.

I cleared my throat.
Did you know my dad's in jail?

Junior's eyebrows went up.
Really? What for?

I smirked.
Something big.

Like what?

Get me a Coke and I'll tell you all about it.

What He Did

I took my time
opening the can,
having my first sip.

Well?
said Junior.

I wiped my lips
with the back of my hand
and looked Junior
right in the eye.

He killed someone.

It wasn't a lie.

For real? Why didn't you ever tell me?

I shrugged.
You never asked.

After the Storm

Grab your coat, Jett.
The ocean had a bellyache
last night and, this morning,
it threw up on the beach.

Threw up what?

Sea glass, I hope.

Sounds like it was really SEAsick.
Get it, Grandma? SEAsick?
Because it's the sea
and it's sick?

I get it, Jett. I get it.
The poor thing had WAVES of nausea all night long.

Within five minutes,
Grandma was pumping her fist.
Yes! Seafoam green!

All I found
was a tiny piece
of a broken beer bottle.
Its sharp tip
pricked my finger.
When I saw the tiny
bubble of blood,
I pricked my thumb, too.

I sat on the shoreline.
I'll do them all, I thought.
All ten.

But then,
out of the corner of my eye,
a heart-shaped rock.

I picked it up.
A perfect fit in my palm.

Grandma!

I dropped the glass
and ran down the beach.

For you.

She said,
Jett, you really are a kind boy.

And I almost believed her.

Old

We walked home slowly,
skipping stones along the way.
One of my stones
skipped across the surface
of the water six times.

Grandma said,
I skipped ten once.

Yeah, I said. *You told me.*

She laughed.
Old people repeat themselves.

You're not old.

I'm seventy-three!

One hundred is old,
I said.
You're not old.
You're not old at all.

I guess I figured if I said it enough,
we'd both believe it.

The Find

Here, Grandma. Try this one.

I reached for it,
the perfect skimmer,
then,
as I picked it up,
a shiver.
Between the rocks below,

a shiny speck of blue.

With fingers like pincers
I reached for my prey.

In,
pinch,
pull.

Grandma!

Her eyes lit up.
A marble!

A ... marble?
I thought it was sea glass.

Grandma held it to the light.
It IS sea glass.
My favorite kind.
A marble,
lost by a child
a long time ago.
Just imagine how old this is!

She placed it
in my palm.

This,
she said,
is very, very special.

I rolled it
between my pincers.

*Grandma? Is it okay if I don't add this
to the pickle jar?*

*It's yours, Jett.
You can do whatever you want with it.*

I wasn't sure what I wanted to do with it.
So I put it in the deepest corner
of my pants pocket
for safekeeping.

That Bird

When we got home,
I showed my marble to Horace.

Look what I found, Birdbrain.

Then,
slowly,
meanly,
I rubbed his feathers the wrong way.

Birthday Bonfire

This really is a BONfire.
Get it, Grandma? BONfire?

Huh?

"Bon."
It means "good" in French.

Grandma smiled.
Very clever, Jett.

I squished a marshmallow
onto the end of a stick.

I read the word "clever"
as "cleaver" once.

You did?

Yeah, we were reading Charlotte's Web
and every day Mrs. O'Brien
would pick a student
to read it out loud.
Every day,
in my head,
I'd say,
"Don't pick me,"
but one day she did.
I spoke in a real low voice
and Mrs. O'Brien said,
"Louder."
Then she said,
"Faster."
But the only thing going fast
was my heart.

Then came the line
"You're so clever, Charlotte,"
except I said "cleaver"
and everyone laughed.
So I guess I'm not so clever after all,
am I, Grandma?

The end of my marshmallow
had a big flame on it.
Grandma blew it out.

People are clever in different ways,
Jett.
Take me,
for example.
I did pretty well at school.
I liked reading
and writing
and I was good with numbers.
I had school smarts,
that's for sure,
but did you know
I didn't learn to ride a bike
until I was twelve?
When was it
that you learned again?

I flicked the burned-y bits
of my marshmallow
into the fire.

Four.

Grandma shook her head.
Four. Wow.

Riding a bike isn't clever.

Sure it is,
said Grandma.
So is making witty puns
about bonfires.
Face it, Jett.
You're sharp.
Sharp as a tack.

Actually,
I said,
with a mouthful of fluffy white goo,
I'm as sharp as a cleaver.

Jett Story: Part II

The fire cricked and cracked,
the ocean swished and swooshed,
and, inside my head, a story
steeped,
simmered
and brewed.

Want to hear a Jett story?

Grandma nodded.
Of course.

Once upon a time,
there was a kid named Jett
who blamed a lot of bad stuff
on another kid named Junior.
But everything that happened
wasn't just Junior's fault.
Jett kind of liked being bad.
When him and Junior
were mean to a kid named Colby
and Colby got upset,
Jett felt like he was
winning at something.
And winning,
in the middle of a rotten bad year of losing,
felt good.
But when Jett and Junior were mean
to a big, little man named Alf,
Jett knew he was not a winner.
He was a loser.
A rotten, bad loser.
The biggest loser of all.

I stood up
and poured a pail
of salty ocean water
over the fire.

That's all for now, Grandma.

A Grown Man

I could still smell the bonfire
when I changed out of my clothes
and into pajamas.
The roasty,
toasty,
burned-y smell
was in my hair,
in my eyes
and up my nose.

Alf was afraid of fire.
Once, when a fire truck passed,
its siren blaring,
he put his hands over his ears
and said,
Hot! Hot!

Junior laughed.
He's been scared of fire
since he put his nose
too close to his birthday candles.

I said,
Not all fire is bad, Alf.
If you got lost in the woods
in the middle of winter
a fire could save your life.
Then I added,
But don't you ever try to make a fire, okay, Alf?
Not without help.

Junior always laughed
when I said stuff like that.
Jeez, Jett. He's a grown man.

I hated that.
Alf may have been grown
on the outside,
but on the inside
he was little.

Heavy

Before I went to sleep
I took Nelly's paperweight
out from under my bed.

I said to Duke,
You're a butler, right?
How about you do your job
and return this to Nelly for me?

I imagined him saying,
Right away, sir.

I laid the paperweight on his tray.
Well, go on,
I said,
but he didn't move.

Even in my imagination, I couldn't right this wrong.

Shack

The kids at school said he lived in a shack.
When I heard Colby say it,
I said,
Junior's house might not be a mansion
like yours,
but it's pretty big,
and in the backyard
there's a pool
and a tree house
and a kennel full of puppies.

If I was Pinocchio,
my nose would have poked
Colby's eye out.

You've been to Junior's house?

Of course.
He's my best friend.

I almost wished I was Pinocchio then,
so I could see if my nose would've grown.

Almost Caught in a Lie

Hey, Junior,
said Colby,
what kind of dogs do you have?

I caught Junior's eye and stared at him hard.
Luckily,
surprisingly,
he knew what I meant.

German shepherds,
he said.
Big, mean German shepherds.

My laugh was loud.
Hahaha.
You mean LITTLE German shepherds, right?
They're still puppies, remember?

Well, yeah,
said Junior,
but they're big puppies.

Cool,
said Colby.
They're one of my favorite breeds.

Later, Junior said,
What the heck, Jett?

He said you lived in a shack.
It made me mad.
So I told him you had a pool
and a kennel full of puppies.

It … made you mad?

Well, yeah.

Jett?

Yeah?

Want to come to my house?

Um, okay.

Just so you know, it really is a shack.

It is?

Yeah, but I know you won't tell.
It can't be any more embarrassing
than having a father in jail.

Home Sweet Home

We walked through
the downtown area
past coffee shops
and restaurants
and ended up
in a neighborhood
of small brick houses.
Some were neat and tidy
with bright-colored shutters
and pots full of flowers
on the porch.
Others had old cars
parked on overgrown lawns
and screen doors
hanging off their hinges.

I figured Junior's house
would be an
"old car on the lawn"
kind of house
so I was surprised
when we turned into
one of the neat and tidy ones.

This isn't a shack,
I said.

Junior walked past
the front door
and headed to the back.

A big wooden shed
filled a corner of the backyard.

Home sweet home.

Junior's Stash

Two beds,
one on each side,
a curtain hung down the middle.

Who lives here?

Me and my dad.

So who lives in the house?

Aunt Cora and Alf.

He pulled a box
out from under his bed.

Want some?

Some what?

He raised the box,
then tipped it.

Food rained down in miniature.

Samples

He offered me a beef stick
the size of my pinkie.

Where did you get all this stuff?

The big supermarket down the road.
They give it out, free.
You're supposed to have an adult with you,
but I just help myself when nobody's looking.

I picked up a small rectangle of cheddar.
Shouldn't this be in the fridge?

What are you, the food police?

If I was the food police,
I'd have made sure Junior's food was full-size.

Aunt Cora

Do you even have a fridge?

No.

What about a bathroom?

We go inside for that.
Meals, too, supposedly.
But Aunt Cora hates me
so I pretty much survive on my samples.

Why does she hate you?

Because my mom is her sister
and when she ran away
and never came back
Aunt Cora blamed my dad.

Why?

Because he didn't treat my mom too good.

How is that your fault?

I dunno. But it must be, partly anyway.
After Mom left, Aunt Cora said,
"Maybe if you weren't in so much trouble all the time,"
dot dot dot.

She said "dot dot dot"?

No, but you know what I mean.
Anyway, she only offered us this place
because she said Mom would've wanted a roof
over my head.

I looked out the small shed window
toward the house.

THAT roof would be better.

Mask

This was Aunt Cora's box,
from Halloween.
I found it in the recycling.
She gave out mini chocolate bars.
I went to her door six times.
She didn't recognize me in my mask.

What were you?

A robber.

A robber?
Why don't you ever play cops and robbers
with me and Alf?

Because I'm not five.

I'm not, either.

You act like it.

Shut up, Junior.

No, you shut up.

WHY DON'T YOU BOTH SHUT UP?

Junior's Dad

We didn't hear the door open,
but there he was,
Junior's dad,
filling the shed
with cigarette smoke.

Hello, son.

Junior stood up to leave.

Where do you think you're going?

His voice was a whisper.
Out.

What's that, son?
Can't hear you.

Junior's cheeks went red.
Out.

Who's your friend?

Jett. From school.

His father smirked.
From School is a weird last name.

Junior nodded toward the door.
Come on, Jett.

His father blocked the way.
You forgot to say "excuse me."

Junior's shoulders slumped.
Excuse me.

His father's jaw pulsed, like a heart.
You forgot to say "please."

Junior looked to the floor.
Please.

His dad grinned.
Pretty please.

I knew it wasn't possible,
but I could've sworn I saw Junior shrink.

Pretty please.

Laughter.
With sugar on top.

Junior's voice was so small,
I shrunk a bit, too.
With sugar on top.

On our way out
he grabbed Junior's arm.
If you wanted to have a friend over,
you should have asked first.

The Empty Store

Running,
fast as lightning,
the sound of my own heart
beating in my ears,
my breath going
huh-huh-huh.

Over fences,
down alleys,
through the window
of a boarded-up store.

What is this place?

No answer,
just a stare —

a
blank
empty
zombie
stare.

Michael

Sitting on the counter,
eyes on the floor.
Quiet,
for loads of minutes,
until:

We're both named Michael.
That's why I'm called Junior.
When I'm eighteen,
I can change my name.
Legally.
When I'm eighteen,

I can be someone new.

New Name

Who would you be?

I dunno.
Who do I look like?

I hopped up next to him,
gave his face
a good once-over.
Browny-gold eyes,
shiny and wet
like pebbles on the beach.
Freckles,
like a million
grains of sand.

How about Finley?
(It was the first thing
that popped into my head.)

Junior pushed me off the counter.
That's the stupidest name I ever heard.

I rubbed my arm,
smiling,
grateful that the zombie was gone.

Make Believe

An old cash register,
working but empty.

Junior played with the buttons.
Ding!
If this was full of money,
I'd run away
and start a new life.

Poor Junior.
Didn't he know
that fresh starts weren't
what they were cracked up to be?

Ding!
Let's play store.

Are you joking?
Junior hated pretend.

Ding!
You be the cashier
and I'll be the customer.
Then we'll switch.

We bought:
cereal
granola bars
toilet paper
ice cream
Coke
chocolate
pork chops
milk

We called each other "sir"
and, sometimes, even
"madam."

Come again soon!
See you next time!
Have a great day now, ya hear?

We played all day
till I had to go.
Sorry, my money's all spent.

Wait, Jett,
there's no need to go.
I accept IOUs.

J&J's

We called our store J&J's.

Jett and Junior's!

No, Junior and Jett's!

It was where we spent all our time.

I could live here,
said Junior.

Where would you sleep?
I asked.

Junior looked around.
Anywhere.

It was our little secret,
J&J's —

mostly because Junior said
he'd punch my lights out
if I told anyone.

Still My Father

Grandma mentioned
the penitentiary
again
and I said,
I'm not visiting no jail,
and she said,
Did you know a double negative
makes a positive?
and I said,
What's that supposed to mean?
and she said,
If you're not visiting "no jail"
you must be visiting "some jail,"
and I yelled,
I'm not visiting some jail!
I'm not visiting any jail!
Grandma sighed.
He's still your father, Jett.
People make mistakes.

I was so mad,
I ran out the door.

Mistakes?
I said to the ocean.
She calls THAT a mistake?

The ocean roared.

My Father's Mistake

A red minivan
bashed to bits.

The father,
the girl,
the baby,
the boy —
killed on Harrington Road.

And the Mother

The mother, too,
who didn't die …

but wished she had.

Cookies

Grandma,
blue hair blowing in the wind,
a plate of gingersnaps in her hands.

The tide's coming in, Jett.
You'll be swimming back soon.

I didn't argue.
It wasn't because I was afraid
of being stuck on the lion,
but because Grandma's cookies
were the best in the world.

Cookies with Alf

I made cookies with Alf once.
It wasn't planned.
Junior and me were
heading to the shed
(our pockets full of samples)
when he saw us.

He called from the house:
Jett Plane help?

I said,
With what?
but I knew it was baking —
he had flour on his nose.

Aunt Cora invited me in.

Junior followed behind.

Sliced Down the Middle

She gave me a wooden spoon —
Junior, a nudge to the corner.

You're always in the way.

While Alf and me stirred,
Junior stared at his feet.

It was like being sliced
right down the middle.
I was in two pieces
and all I wanted
was to be one again.

I said,
Junior, do you want to add the chocolate chips?

Okay.

Not with those dirty hands!

The pieces of me that were
splitting in two
kept splitting
and splitting
until I was
chopped down
to a tiny fleck of myself.

I wanted to say,
Why can't he help?
but flecks don't have much
of a voice.

Alf's Room

Jett Plane come see my room?

A track on the floor,
in the shape of an eight.
His trains lined up,
neat and tidy.

Thomas
Donald
Duncan
Edward
Rosie

Junior appeared in the doorway.
Come on, Jett.
Let's go.

A stuffed bear on the bed.
This is Bear.

That's real cute, Alf,
I said.

Squeeze him, Jett Plane.

Soft.

Look! I have train curtains.

They were blue and white
and through them
I could see Junior's shed.

Nice.

He patted his bed.
Sit.

I sat.
You have a real nice room, Alf.

He showed me his policeman doll.
This is Tective.

He's cool.

Want to see my money?

Junior let out a sigh.

Sure, Alf.
But this is the last thing, okay?

Alf's smile took up
the whole of his face.

He took a briefcase
from under his bed.
It was brown leather
with a combination lock built in.

Junior laughed.
There's no money in that case.

Alf took some paper out of a drawer.
Secret numbers.

Junior rolled his eyes.

Alf turned the dials slowly,
checking and rechecking the code.
Then, thumbs on the buttons,

push.

The clasps didn't open.

He tried again.

Junior reached for the numbers.
Let me try, stupid.

Alf hid them behind his back.

Junior flopped on the bed.

Whatever.
There's no money
in that stupid case anyway.

Alf passed the paper to me.
Jett Plane help.

I turned the dials —
four,
eight,
three —
then took a step back.

It should work now, Alf. Press the buttons.

The clasps unsnapped with a *POP!*
Want to see the money that Jenny gave me?

Junior sat up.
What did you say?

Who's Jenny?
I asked.

My mother,
said Junior.

No,
said Alf.
Jenny's my sister.

Junior growled.
She's both,
you stupid dummy.

Leave him alone, Junior.

Maybe he should leave me *alone,*
going on about how rich he is all the time
with my mother's money.

I shrugged.
It's not Alf's fault
she gave money to him
and not to you.

Junior eyed the case.
If you ask me,
that money is technically mine.

How do you figure that?
I asked.

My mother.
My money.

Alf snapped the clasps shut.
My money.

Cora came to say the cookies
were ready.
Don't they smell great?

Junior said,
They smell like dog crap.

Cora's face went red with anger.
Out of my house.
Now.

I left, too.

Junior was shrinking again
and I wanted to help
make him big.

Blue Quilted Bag

We ran to J&J's.
Behind the counter,
a blue quilted sleeping bag.
Junior wriggled down into it.

Where did that come from?

Stole it. From Cora.

I sat on the corner.
Have you … slept here?

Once.

He lay on his side,
his head on his folded arm.

Junior?
What was it like before your mom left?

We didn't live in a shed.
When he wasn't home
she'd sing,
all the time, singing.
Then,
she left.

A lump in my throat.
She just … left?

Said she was going
to the hairdresser's.
I was reading a comic.
I barely looked up.
She didn't leave me a briefcase of money.

I'm sorry, Junior.

Junior wriggled out of the bag
and sat up straight.

Just like that,

big again.

Why?

We leaned against the wall
and pulled the sleeping bag
over our laps.

I never even knew my mother had money.

*Maybe she saved it up,
for a really long time.*

*But why give it to Alf?
Why not me?*

*Maybe because Alf is,
you know,
special.
He'll never be able to get a job
and make money.
Not like you.
When you're older you can look
after yourself.*

*But I need money now.
And lots of it.*

What for?

*I want to move out.
I want to run away
and never come back.
Just like she did.*

Where would you go?

*This could be my home.
When I slept here last week,
I thought I'd be scared,
but I'm scareder at home,
with my dad.*

I could live here, Jett.
I just need money,
for food,
a flashlight,
a pillow, maybe.

I'd never really touched Junior before,
but I put an arm around his shoulder.

I said,
Maybe
we should tell someone.

Telling

I did.
Last week,
after I punched Charlie Tate.
I told Mrs. Brooks I was tired
and I snapped.
She said,
"Being tired is no excuse
for hitting someone."
But I was more than tired, Jett.
His whistling,
his high-pitched whistling,
it was like someone was drilling
right into my brain.
So I told her.
I told her that sometimes
my dad wakes me at night,
keeps me up for hours,
yelling about my mom,
blaming me.
She said,
"You have to be careful,
making an accusation like that.
An accusation like that
could get you removed
from the home."
And I thought,
"Good. Mission accomplished."
But then she said something
about foster care
and I got scared.
So when she said,

"Now, I'll ask you again,
why did you hit Charlie?"
I said,
"Because he's a doofus."
I told her I made
the rest of it up.

Because
what if being
in foster care is worse
than living
with my dad?

I'll Help

I'll help you move into J&J's
and I won't tell anyone.
I'll ask for seconds after supper
and deliver them to you every night.
I'll bring you your schoolwork
so when you are older
you can get a job
and move to a better place.
Everything will be okay, Junior.
I promise.
You can count on me.

Asleep Again

His head
against my shoulder,
his breath
getting deep.

Junior,
asleep again
at J&J's.

Very Smart, Indeed

Grandma decided to cook a meal
for everyone at the stinky house.
She also decided
that I would help ...
whether I wanted to
or not.

Nelly and her friends deserve a good meal,
don't you think, Jett?

I thought of Junior's samples.
Everyone deserves good food.

Grandma put on The Beatles
and sang "Octopus's Garden"
while she chopped.

Hey, Grandma, how many tickles
does it take to make an octopus laugh?

She held her knife still as she thought.
Hmmm ... I give up.

Ten tickles.

Grandma roared.

I had an INKling
you'd find that funny.

She wiped her eyes.
Stop it, Jett.
I'll never get this lasagna made
at this rate.

I said,
Octopuses don't actually
have tentacles, you know.

Still,
it's always handy
to be ARMed with
an octopus joke.
Get it, Grandma? ARMed?
Because octopuses have arms, not tentacles.

Grandma passed me a bowl.
Get to work, Jett.
How about you KRAKEN an egg
into this ricotta?

Hey, I actually got that!

What do you mean "actually"?

I'm not that smart, that's all.
But I know that the kraken
is a mythological creature
that looks like a giant squid.
Me and Alf read all about it.
Did you know that squid
and octopuses
are called cephalopods?

If eyes could talk
hers would have said,
I love you.

Jett, have you heard yourself?

I KRAKENed the egg on the side of the bowl.
Of course.
I have ears.

Then you should know that you are smart.
Very smart, indeed.

I got a D in math.
And my spelling's bad.

Doesn't matter.
You're clever as a fox.
Trust me.
In this life,
that counts for something.

So,
you think,
when I grow up,
I can be someone?

Grandma's face went soft.
You ARE someone, dear.
You're my Jett.

One Wish

She put the lasagna
in the oven
and while it cooked
I stared at the pickle jar,
imagining
that the sea glass inside
had magical powers —
one wish
and summer would last
forever.
I put my hands on the jar
and closed my eyes.
I wish —

B-e-e-e-e-e-p!

Lasagna's done, Jett!
Time to go.

I never did finish the wish.

Eight, All Together

We sat around a table
on chairs that didn't match.
Me,
Grandma,
Nelly,
the guy with the darting eyes,
the guy with the ripped pants,
a short old man in a baseball cap,
a lady in a ball gown
and a man who looked like Santa
(except his beard was yellow).

Nelly bowed her head.
Gob is gwabe.
Gob is goob.

A laugh —
heh-heh-heh —
from the ripped-pants guy.

Grandma, loudly,
with Nelly:
Let us thank Him for our food.

Through the meal:

Ball Cap Guy shouting, *Cheers!*

Ball Gown Lady singing, *Shall we dance?*

Ripped Pants Guy going, *heh-heh-heh.*

Darting Eyes Guy … darting his eyes.

Smelly Nelly —
Nelly —
gumming her food.

Santa
didn't
say
a
word.

Then, Grandma:

My oh my, who is this?
Pitter-pattering,
around her feet,
a tiny bundle of fluff.

Santa:
She's been hanging around here for weeks.

A beard like Santa,
but a voice like Scrooge,
not a hint of jolly at all.

I scooped her up.
What's her name?

Snow White.

Weird name for a black dog.

A million puppy kisses,
two paws on my chest
and one —
only one —
pressing into my lap.

Seemed like everyone was broken
in the stinky house.

If I Had a Camera

If I had a camera
I'd have taken a picture
of Snow White
and sent it to Alf,
even though
he said he'd rather have
a pet elephant
than a pet dog.

When I asked why, he'd said,
Elephants are big.

Truth was,
Alf loved animals
no matter their size.

We found a centipede once,
outside McEwan's store.
We watched it for ages
until Junior came along

and stepped on it.

Proud

Ball Cap Guy said I looked like his grandson,
a straight-A student,
the football team captain,
a national spelling bee winner.
His picture was in the paper and everything.

I knew what Grandma would say about me.

He's got a way with words, my Jett.
He's clever as a fox.

Nelly

Nelly's eyes,
soft and kind,
on Snow White.

Want to hold her?
I asked.

Nelly's eyes,
hard and mad,
on me.

Go abay.

Bank Robber

That night,
a dream:
a mask on my face
a NO REGRETS plan
my finger out like a gun
Nelly in the way
in front of the bank

spare change
spare change

bang! bang!
until she is dead
my finger-gun smoking and hot

a briefcase of bills
a getaway car
a beer at the stinky house
clinking glasses
with Ball Cap Guy
laughing
shouting
cheers!

Only a Dream

I told myself
it was only a dream.
Trouble was,
it felt as real as
the thump of my heart.

The floor creaked
as I got out of bed,
so I sat down
and stood up again.
Creak!
Again and again —
Creak!
Creak!
— hoping Grandma would wake.

I wished for daylight,
when dreams
were only dreams.

Hey, Duke,
do you think I'm too old
to go wake Grandma?

No, sir. I do not.

Outside her room,
Grandma?

The door whipped open.
Jett?

I had a bad dream.

How about some cocoa?

Turns out
it's not just daylight
that makes dreams
only dreams.

Cocoa

Grandma?

Yes?

This cocoa tastes different.

Different good or different bad?

Just different.

Probably because I eyeballed it.

You didn't measure?

Never do.

You should.
That way you always know
what you're going to get.

What's the fun in that?

Ebb & Flow

Grandma?

Yes?

Why can't things just stay the same?

Because life is like the tides.
In, out.
Back, forth.
Push, pull.
High, low.
You just have to go with the flow, you know?

Yeah …

Grandma?

Yes?

Want to hear a story?

Jett Story: Part III

There once was a boy
who was tired of being poor,
so one day he said to his friend Jett,
"I'm gonna steal a whole load of money
and you're gonna help."

Grandma listened
to every bit —
the beginning,
the end,
the stuff in between.

My poor Jett,
she said.

No Regrets

Junior, I'm just not sure …

You said I could count on you.

Not if it means stealing from Alf.

Can I show you something?

Slowly,
carefully,
he lifted his shirt.

I wondered,
how was I still alive?

Because my heart had stopped beating.

When I Could Breathe Again

When I could breathe again,
I asked,
Does it hurt?

Junior ran his fingers across
the purple-y yellowish bruises.
No, it tickles.

Why would your dad do that?

The same reason your dad's in jail.
Some people are just born bad,
I guess.

Robin Hood

I am Robin Hood.
I steal from the rich
and give to the poor.

While They Were at Church

Sunday morning,
under Alf's window.

Don't you have a key?
I asked.

I'm only allowed in when she's home.

His arms around my legs.
A boost.
Open it.

A lie.
Can't reach.

A shove.
Try it now.

I can't do this, Junior.

*Open the damn window,
get in the damn house
and open the damn door.*

No.

Please, before my dad wakes up!

I didn't think.
It just happened.
One final no,
then,
quick as a wink,
I thrust my heel
in his gut.

The Kick

I remembered
the bruises
as soon as I did it.
He didn't shout
ouch
or
ow,
but the squeak that he made
was a roar in disguise,
and my own body shook
with his pain.

I opened the window,
easy
as
pie,
and tumbled into the room.

Alf's Room, Uninvited

A butterfly poster
hung on his wall.
His teddy bear,
Bear,
and Tective
on his bed.
Trains on the floor,
all in a row,
a book about dogs
on his desk.

I wondered,
how did Robin Hood sleep at night?

The Lookout

I pulled the curtain
away from the glass,
my lookout eyes
on the road.

Jett! I can't find his secret numbers.

They're in his bedside table.

No, they're not.

A little glass elephant
on the window ledge,
his trunk
curled upward,
reaching.

Jett, what's the code?

I whispered it to the elephant:

Four,
eight,
three.

He promised not to tell.

Dishonesty

Elephants can't see very well,
but are really good smellers.

I read that
in a book with Alf.

Jett? The code?

Alf said if he had an elephant
he'd feed it peanuts
out of his hand.

Jett! The code!

But the book also said
elephants don't actually
like peanuts.

I made sure to skip that page.

Jett!

Elephants are
loyal,
strong
and smart.

JETT!

Okay, okay!
Four ...
six ...
three.

The book said nothing
about elephants lying.

Guilt

It's not working! The code's not working!

It is a well-known fact
that elephants feel emotions,
like
joy,
love,
grief.

Oh my God.
It's not working!
It's not working!

I wondered if they ever felt guilt.

Jett?
Can you help?
Please?

Coming.

Crash

The curtain?
A breeze?
My leg?
Something
sent the elephant
crashing
to the floor.

Whatever that was,
leave it,
called Junior.
We're running out of time.

Sweat on Junior's forehead,
the briefcase on the bed.

You try, Jett.

Bear and Tective,
staring,
eyes on my shaking hands.

Turn the stupid dials, Jett!

Then,
a cry,
like a hurt animal
caught in a trap.

Jett Plane?

Down

My heart sank
as low as it could go.
Down to my toes,
through my shoes,
into the floorboards,
all the way down,
down
down
down
to hell.

Alf ... I ...

His eyes,
big,
brown
and wide,
staring at my hands
on the dials
of his briefcase.

Alf, I ...

I looked to Junior
for help,
but Junior's eyes,
squinty and mean,
were on Alf.

Why aren't you at church?

Too loud.

What do you mean "loud"? Church isn't loud.

Alf's forehead wrinkled.
The singing.

All I wanted
was to see Alf smile.

I said,
I know a joke about singing.

Junior scowled.
Shut up, Jett.

Why are pirates great singers?

Junior moved to the window.
Come on, let's go.
Before Cora comes.

I stepped in front of Alf,
tilted my head to catch his eye.

Because they can hit the high Cs.

He looked up.
Jett Plane take my money?

The room,
the world,
my insides,
everything,

spinning.

Grab the case, Jett, let's go.

I looked to the window.
Through it,
Junior's shed.

I closed my eyes.
NO REGRETS.

I tucked the case under my arm
and climbed through the window,

no looking back.

The Briefcase

I laid it on the counter at J&J's.

Open it, Jett.

Alf's voice in my head.
Jett Plane take my money?

But there was no going back now.
I turned the dials.

Four,
eight,
three.

I let Junior pop the clasps.

A dent in his cheek,
a dimple,
that I'd never noticed before.

Finally!

When he opened the lid,
it was like a wave
washed over him,

wiping out all his hope.

Junior? What is it?

His voice was a whisper.
Monopoly money.

Not a Grown Man

Junior's fists,
tight around the paper bills.
That stupid retard.

A wave over me then, too,
all my sympathy
for Junior Dawson
washed away.

Shut up, Junior.
None of this is Alf's fault.

He lied.
He said my mother gave him money.

She did give him money.
Play money.

Play money.
He's a grown man.

Stop saying that.

Saying what?

That he's a grown man.
You always say that.
As if he should be able to do anything.
Well, he can't.
Can't you see?
Alf is special.

The Freak-out

Trust me, Jett!
I know he's special!
He gets everything he wants!
Always has!
Always will!

When Junior opened the case
he had been as white as a ghost.
Now he was red,
like
the devil.
Bills went flying,
across the counter,
over the floor.

Calm down, Junior!

No!
I won't calm down!
He gets everything.
And I get nothing.
I live in a shack, Jett.
A shack!

I never knew
the devil could cry.

I started to tidy the bills.
I'll ask my mom
if you can stay with us.
Maybe, if I explain —

No.
I need to go
where my dad won't find me.
I want to live at J&J's.
But I can't now.
Because Alf ruined it.
Alf ruined everything.

I was about to say
that Alf ruined nothing —
he said he had money
and he did.
It was fake, that was all.
I was about to say
all of these things,
but before I could

Junior ran out the door.

No Heart, After All

Stop!
Junior!
Where are you going?

But I knew.
In the pit of my stomach,
I knew.

I chased him
the whole way back
to his aunt's house.

Alf was still in his room,
staring at the open window.

I grabbed Junior by the arm,
held him back.

But Junior was strong.

You lied, retard. You're not rich!

Alf,
knocked to the ground,

Junior,
on Alf's chest,
yelling,
punching,

so much punching.

Alf,
crying,
scared,
confused,
his eyes on mine,
saying,
HELP.

Me,
frozen,
paralyzed,
scared.

Please, st— st—

Dry mouth,
sick stomach,
eyes blurring.

Eyes blurring
to blackness.
Was I dead?
Maybe I was.
I had no heart, after all.
It fell right through the floorboards.

My cheek,
stinging and hot,
Junior's face in mine.

Jett! We have to get out of here.

Did you ... slap me?

I was on the floor,
next to Alf.
Alf curled into a ball,
whimpering.

We can't just leave him.

Junior,
at the window.
Watch me.

A Million, Trillion Pieces

I knelt over him,
shook him by the shoulder.

Alf! Talk to me!

He rolled over.

His face,
bloody and bruised.

If I'd had a heart
it would have broken
into a million, trillion pieces.

I collapsed,
my head on his chest,
crying.

I'm sorry.
I'm sorry.
I'm sorry.

Aunt Cora in the doorway.
What in heaven's name?
She fell to her knees.
What happened?

Alf lifted his head.

Jett Plane took my money.

How Could You?

She called a doctor,

then the police.

How could you, Jett?

I didn't. Junior —

You didn't take his money?

Well, yeah, but it was Junior who …
I would never, ever …

Were you here when it happened?

Yeah, but —

You know what, Jett?
Save it for the police.

Doctor Butt

Alf giggled through his tears.
Doctor Butt?

That's my name.

She was gentle with him.
Talking him through every move.

Now, I'm just going to touch your nose ...
shine a light in your eyes ...
dab this cut with some cream.

With every *ouch*,
Cora looked at me
as if to say,

See? See what you've done?

Not Rich Anymore

Funny, he seemed to care
more about his money
than his face.

I'm not rich anymore.

Cora kissed the top of his head.
We'll get your money back, hon.

Bang Bang

While Cora talked to the police,
Alf sat next to me,
tears on his cheeks,
his hands clasped in his lap.

I said,
You were never supposed to know it was us.

As if that made it okay.

He rocked back and forth.

Alf? Please talk to me.

Slowly,
sadly,
his finger uncurled.

*Bang bang, Jett Plane,
you're dead.*

Warning

Junior in the back of a police car,
returned to the scene of the crime.

Alf ride in police car, too?

Sure, Alf.
Right after I talk to these boys.

Junior,
forced to sit next to me.
Snitch.

I wondered if we'd ever see J&J's again.

My mother,
in tears.

Junior's dad,
in a fit of anger.

Together,
Junior and me
were asked
question,
after question,
after question.

Junior lied
and denied.

I told everything.

It was a shock,
when he was taken away,
silver handcuffs
around his wrists.

He was just a kid.

I wanted to say,
Hey, Junior? Do you have regrets now?
But I didn't.

I got a warning.
Next time, there'll be consequences.

My voice, a whisper.
There'll be no next time.

Alf's voice,
as my mother
dragged me out the door:
Jett not my friend anymore.

I knew then
that I had a heart
because a terrible pain
shot right through it.

We Are the Champions

A dream:
the crouching lion
floating away,
Alf and Nelly on top.
My own voice
waking me up.
Come back!
Come back!

It was three in the morning,
but I went downstairs

to check that the lion was there.

Grandma appeared behind me.
Can't sleep?

Weird dream.

She put on the cocoa;
the radio, too.

Grandma?

Mm-hmm?

I'm not a very good person.

How could that be
when I love you so much?

A light on the waves
in the distance.

"We Are the Champions"
came on the radio.
The singers sang it
over and over,
like they were convincing themselves,
like if they said it enough
it might come true.

The light on the waves,
sill glowing.
I wondered,
did the captain ever make mistakes?
Did he think about them
out there in the dark
in the middle of the night?

I stared at the chocolate sludge
at the bottom of my mug.
It was thick
and dark
like mud.

When I next looked up,

the light in the ocean was gone.

Fighting till the End

Grandma's voice,
drifting from her bedroom,
singing
about champions and friends
and a fight to the end.

And in my head,
I sang along,
over
and
over
and over again.

The First Step

Grandma?
Can I make a phone call?

Her eyes brightened.
You calling your dad?

I practically bit her head off.
No!

Then who?

Alf.

You sure you're ready for that?

I want to make things better.

She smiled.
Well, a phone call is a good first step.

As I dialed the number
I wondered,

what exactly was I stepping toward?

Courage

Cora?
It's me, Jett.

Silence.

I was wondering,
is it okay —
would I be able to —

The sound of her breathing,
light and quick.

I made a mistake, I know.
A big one.
I just …
Can't I just have
a second chance?

Seconds ticking by
1, 2, 3, 4, 5, 6 …

Cora?

If you upset him —

I won't.

Tick
Tick
Tick

Alf, hon! Can you come here?

A Conversation

His gigantic *hello,*
the most awesome
sound in the world.

Hi, Alf. It's Jett.

Silence.

I, uh, just wanted to say hi.

I listened hard
for the sound of his
breath.

I've missed you, Alf.

Tick
Tick
Tick

Jett Plane?

Happiness,
filling me
like a balloon.

Yeah?

You need money? I'm rich.

Pop!

Sadness,
exploding everywhere.

No.
I don't need money.

Jett Plane?

Yeah?

Guess what?

What?

Elephants don't like peanuts.

A laugh.
Inflated again.

Jett Plane?

Yes?

I have a budgie.

I pictured it —
big, gentle Alf,
a little bird
on his finger.

Budgie has no name.
I can't think of one.

How about Horace?

Alf laughed and laughed.

How about ...
Hmmm, let's see ...
Sky?

Laughing again.

Jett Plane?

Yeah?

I'm not mad anymore.

I didn't know
whether to laugh or to cry,
so I did both,

silently.

Jett Plane?

I'm here.

Cora wants to talk now.

Okay.

Bye-bye, Jett Plane.

Bye-bye, Alf.

Not All Bad

Well, Jett,
seems we could all learn a lot from Alf.

He's the best person I know.

He sure is.

Cora?
Can I ask you a question?

Yes?

How's Junior?

He lives in the country now.
With his aunt Mary.

I just wanted to say ...
what he did,
it was terrible,
but he's ... he's not all bad.

Well, Jett,
we'll just have to agree to disagree on that one.

Applesauce

She said,
That boy is going to end up just like his father.
The apple doesn't fall far from the tree, you know.

I pictured an apple,
battered and bruised.

I said,
He didn't deserve to live in a shed.

Jett, you know I couldn't let them live in my house —
that man wasn't safe to be around.

All she had to do was pick him up,
but she stepped on him instead.

Poor Junior,
he got squished to bits.

The Ticket

On Duke's tray, a plane ticket,
a reminder,
a paper whisper from Grandma:

It'll soon be time to go.

Nobody's Perfect

Duke? Everyone I know
has done something wrong.
Even Grandma.

Nobody's perfect, sir.

I think I might go see my dad.

Silence.

I guess he wasn't too sure, either.

Different

Grandma?
Will I look different to him?

You're bigger, that's for sure.
But don't worry, he'll recognize you.
Even with your blue hair.

I held the pickle jar up to the light.
Can people tell if you've changed on the inside?

Depends on the person, I guess.
Some people, it seems, can look right into your soul.

I smiled.
Like you.

She smiled back.
Yes. Like me.
And, trust me, Jett,

your soul's a good one.

The Visit

The guards called me "buddy,"
said my blue hair was cool.

Mind if we look in your pockets?

I dug down deep.

Cool marble, buddy.

A walk through the metal detector.

Don't worry. It's just like at the airport.

No.
At the airport,
people are going places.

Down a long hall,
their keys
a countdown,
a jingle
a jangle
with every step,

5
4
3
2

Wait!

Yes?

Will I see other prisoners?

Just your dad.

Jingle-jangle,
key in the keyhole,
the creak of the door
opening wide.

Hi, Jett.

A Table Between Us

A table between us,
a guard at the door,
a camera
high in the corner.

How was your year on the mainland?

Rotten and bad, I thought.

Good, I said.

I'm glad, Jett.

Silence.

I saw a whale last week.

Boy, was I lame.

Orca?

Humpback.

I dug down deep.
Look what I found.

Lucky.

Want to hold it?

My father's hand,
the high-fiver,
the head-patter,
the ball-catcher,
the tear-wiper,
stretched out in front of me,
big
and
strong.

I dropped the marble into it.

He rolled it between his fingers.
I missed you, Jett.

I missed him, too.

I'm going back to the mainland tomorrow.

He passed the marble back,
his fingers around mine,
just for a second.

Have a great year, Jett.

I'll try,
I said.

And I meant it.

Time to Pack

My suitcase,
open,
at the end of my bed.

Inside,
a fossil,
a whale bone,
a piece of red sea glass.

I stared at them through blurry eyes.

Later, Grandma said,
Now, Jett,
when you board that plane tomorrow
let's not say goodbye,
let's say toodle-oo,
it's so much cheerier.

One More Thing

The next day,
toodle-oo
to the crouching lion,
toodle-oo
to Duke.
Goodbye
to Horace.

On the way to the airport:
Grandma,
would it be okay
if I said goodbye to Nelly?

She delivered me right to her door.

Can I go up alone?

Of course.

Back Where It Belonged

She offered me her only chair,
the one with the rip
down the middle.

You sit, Nelly.

I took the paperweight
out of my pocket.

I took this.
I don't have a reason.
I just did it.
I'm sorry.

I held it out.

Nelly's hands
stayed in her lap.

I put the paperweight
on the windowsill,
back where it belonged.

There's something else.
I dug down deep.
This was in the ocean.
It got thrown around for a really long time,
by the waves.
That's why it's so smooth and frosty.

Nelly strained to see it.

I moved closer.

It's a marble, see?
It went through a
really tough time
when it was in the ocean,

but in the end
it came out like this.
I thought you'd like it.
Because it's glass
like your paperweight.

Nelly let me place it into her palm.

Anyway, I gotta go.
Maybe I'll see you next summer.

Gob besh you,
she said,
Gob besh you.

Toodle-oo

Grandma and me
in the airport.

Well, Jett,
it's a nice, clear day for flying.

Yep.

It'll be good to be back, won't it?
Back into your routine?

Yep.

And school starts soon.
New school, right?

Yep. Junior high.

A fresh start.

I said,
You know, fresh starts aren't always
what they're cracked up to be.

Grandma said,
This will be different.

I smiled.
I know.

THIS IS YOUR BOARDING ANNOUNCEMENT
FOR FLIGHT 778.

We knew it was coming.
It was what we'd been waiting for.
But we weren't ready.

I rushed into Grandma's arms.
I'll miss you.

I'll miss you, too, Jett.

One last hug,
one last whisper.
I gave Nelly the marble.
I think she really liked it.

Of course she did.
It's a gem, Jett.
Just like you.

Toodle-oo, Grandma.

Toodle-oo, Jett.

From My Window

From my window:
a puff of blue,
a splash of green,
my cotton candy granny
and her lime-green car.

As the plane took off,
I pictured his face —
sweet and round and covered in stubble.
I couldn't wait to see him.
I'd say,
Guess what, Alf? Jett Plane
was on a jet plane,
and he'd laugh,
a big *ha ha ha,*
and the two of us
would be friends again,
the big, little man

and me.